Wishing on a Bow

Written by Sheila Sweeny Higginson
Illustrated by Loter, Inc.

DISNEY PRESS

New York • Los Angeles

SUSTAINABLE FORESTRY INITIATIVE
Certified Chain of Custody
Promoting Sustainable Forestry
www.sfiprogram.org
SFI-01415
The SFI label applies to the text stock

Minnie's Bow-tique is the busiest business in town.
It seems like everyone wants one of Minnie's beautiful bows.

Ring! Ring! Ring!

Daisy rushes to answer the phone.
"It's Penelope Poodle," Daisy whispers to Minnie.

The famous actress explains that she is going on a big publicity tour for her new movie. She wants to bring a bunch of bows to give to her loyal fans around the world.

"That sounds great!" Minnie says.
"When do you need them?"

"Yesterday," Penelope replies. "But tomorrow will do."

Minnie hangs up the phone and calls her friends over.
"This is our biggest order ever!" she tells them.
"Cuckoo-Loca, get the Bow-matic 3000 ready!"

"Um, lots of luck, Minnie," Cuckoo-Loca says. "We're still waiting for the part to fix the power lever. It won't be here for weeks!"

"Oh, no!" Minnie cries. "What will we do?"

Just then, the doorbell rings. **Ding! Ding!**

"What a pretty package!" calls Daisy. "And look, there's a thank-you note from Madame Ruby. She loved the bows we made for her, Minnie!"

Minnie pulls off the ribbon and opens the box. Inside is a golden lamp with a bow. Minnie carefully takes it out and rubs it with her finger.

A cloud of bright pink smoke fills the Bow-tique.

When the smoke clears, Minnie, Daisy, and Cuckoo-Loca can't believe their eyes!

"Hello, I'm the genie of the lamp. You can call me Teeny."

"Wow!" says Cuckoo-Loca. "They're not kidding when they say big things come in small packages."

"It's nice to meet you, Teeny," Minnie says.
"How can we help you?"

"You already did," Teeny replies. "You released me.
Now I can help you. I will grant you three wishes."

Minnie knows exactly what her first wish will be.
"We have to fill a big new bow order," Minnie says.
"I wish for some helping hands."

"You got it, Minnie!" says Teeny.

Before Minnie can blink, a line of Helping Hands marches into the room.

"Super bow-tastic!" Cuckoo-Loca cheers.

Minnie watches as more Helping Hands march in.

First there are ten.

Then there are twenty.

Then there are hundreds!

Soon there are so many Helping Hands in the Bow-tique, there is no room for Minnie, Daisy, or Cuckoo-Loca!

"I always say three hundred's a crowd!" says Cuckoo-Loca.
"Oh, I wish these Helping Hands would just go away!" Minnie cries.

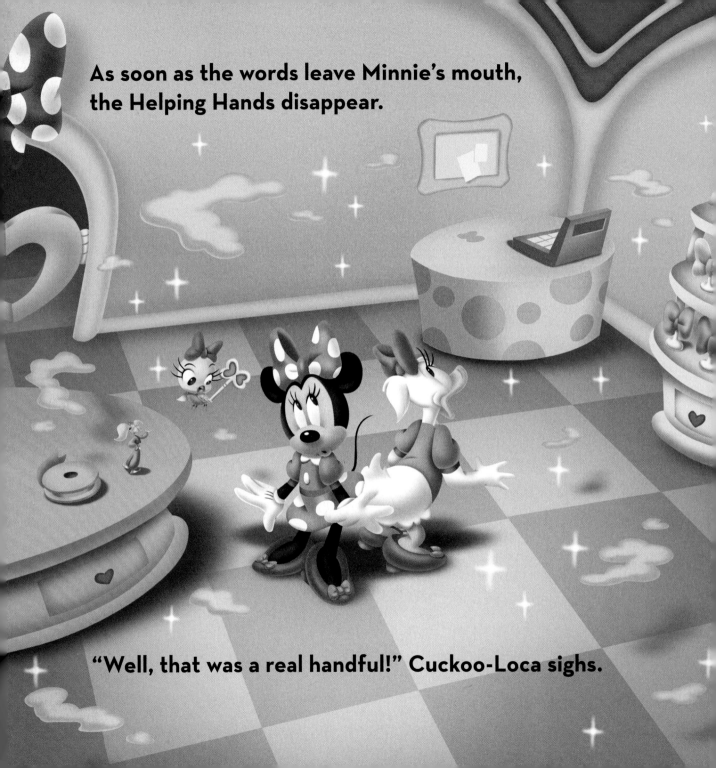

As soon as the words leave Minnie's mouth, the Helping Hands disappear.

"Well, that was a real handful!" Cuckoo-Loca sighs.

"You still have one wish left," Teeny reminds Minnie.

Minnie thinks . . .

and thinks . . .

and thinks some more.

"I think . . .

I have everything I need right here," Minnie says.
"I don't need another wish."

Then Minnie has a great idea.

"Teeny, you can have my wish!" Minnie says.

"You must have seen every wish in the wish book,"
Cuckoo-Loca chirps. "What will you wish for?"

Teeny looks down at her puffy pants and laughs. "I'd love a new outfit," she says. "I've been wearing this one for a thousand years! It's hard to find anything decent in my size."

Minnie takes out a measuring tape and winks at Daisy.
"You don't need to waste a wish on that!" Minnie tells Teeny.
"We've got it covered!"

Daisy measures Teeny.

Minnie draws a pattern.

Cuckoo-Loca finds the fabric.

Snip! Snip! Snap!

"Ta-da!" Minnie calls as she shows off her latest creation.
"Wow!" Teeny says. "It's . . . it's . . ."

"Super bow-tastic!" Cuckoo-Loca says.
"It is!" Teeny agrees.

Teeny goes into the changing room and comes out looking like a brand-new genie!

"Thank you so much," Teeny says. "I've spent a thousand years making other people's dreams come true. No one has ever done anything nice for me! I can't wait to show all my friends!"

Minnie, Daisy, and Cuckoo-Loca wave good-bye.
"I wonder what she'll use her last wish for," Daisy says.

"I wonder how we're going to get all of Penelope's bows finished by tomorrow!" Minnie sighs.

But Minnie doesn't have to wonder. When she goes inside, she sees that Teeny's last wish is truly wonderful! "I guess you got your helping hand after all," Daisy laughs.

"I did," Minnie says. "You see—wishes *do* come true!"